Snow White And the Enormous Turnip

Crabtree Publishing Company
www.crabtreebooks.com
1-800-387-7650

PMB 59051, 350 Fifth Ave.
59th Floor,
New York, NY 10118

616 Welland Ave.
St. Catharines, ON
L2M 5V6

Published by Crabtree Publishing in 2013

For Aoife and Francis

Series editor: Louise John
Editors: Katie Powell, Kathy Middleton
Notes to adults: Reagan Miller
Cover design: Paul Cherrill
Design: D.R.ink
Consultant: Shirley Bickler
Production coordinator and
 Prepress technician: Margaret Amy Salter
Print coordinator: Katherine Berti

Text © Hilary Robinson 2008
Illustration © Simona Sanfilippo 2008

First published in
2008 by Wayland
(A division of Hachette
Children's Books)

Printed in Hong Kong/
092012/BK20120629

**Library and Archives Canada
Cataloguing in Publication**

CIP available at Library and Archives Canada

**Library of Congress
Cataloging-in-Publication Data**

CIP available at Library of Congress

Snow White and the Enormous Turnip

Written by Hilary Robinson
Illustrated by Simona Sanfilippo

Crabtree Publishing Company
www.crabtreebooks.com

Snow White lived in a castle
with her stepmother, the queen,
who had a magic mirror and
was jealous, cruel, and mean.

5

Each day the queen woke up and said,
"Mirror, mirror on the wall,
tell me I'm the prettiest
and the fairest maid of all."

6

7

The magic mirror flashed and said,

"Dear Queen, I tell you true,
Snow White is so much prettier
and far more fair than you."

9

The queen screamed out, "Woodcutter, take this cloak and big, brown hood."

"Leave Snow White to die alone in the heart of Turnip Wood."

11

But the woodcutter loved Snow White.
So he left her at the door
of seven dwarves, who took her in
and loved her even more.

13

Snow White planted seeds and gardened every day.

14

One turnip grew so fat and round
that it stuck fast in the clay.

All the dwarves tugged and pulled.
Snow White's face turned quite pink.

"This turnip's just too big," she said.

"We need more help, I think."

17

At the castle, the jealous queen asked her mirror on the wall, "Am I now the fairest maid?"

"No. Snow White is fairer than you all."

The queen set out to kill Snow White
and thought of a wicked plan.

She dressed herself in a disguise
and down to the wood she ran.

The Seven Dwarves were with Snow White, as she rested by a tree.

"Try a tasty tart," said the queen,
"It'll give you energy."

23

But the apple tart was poisoned,
and Snow White fell to the ground.

The queen was sure her plan had
worked, 'til a prince came riding 'round.

He knelt beside the pale Snow White
and kissed her lovely head.

And when she woke, he helped to pull
the turnip from its bed!

Snow White got married to the prince.

The queen began to cry.

29

And, to celebrate, the dwarves served up an enormous turnip pie!

30

31

Notes for adults

Tadpoles: Fairytale Jumbles are designed for transitional and early fluent readers. The books may also be used for read-alouds or shared reading with younger children.

Tadpoles: Fairytale Jumbles are humorous stories with a unique twist on traditional fairy tales. Each story can be compared to the original fairy tale, or appreciated on its own. Fairy tales are a key type of literary text found in the Common Core State Standards

THE FOLLOWING BEFORE, DURING, AND AFTER READING SUGGESTIONS SUPPORT LITERACY SKILL DEVELOPMENT AND CAN ENRICH SHARED READING EXPERIENCES:

1. Make reading fun! Choose a time to read when you and the child are relaxed and have time to share the story.

2. Before reading, invite the child to preview the book. The child can read the title, look at the illustrations, skim through the text, and make predictions as to what will happen in the story. Predicting sets a clear purpose for reading and learning.

3. During reading, encourage the child to monitor his or her understanding by asking questions to draw conclusions, making connections, and using context clues to understand unfamiliar words.

4. After reading, ask the child to review his or her predictions. Were they correct? Discuss different parts of the story, including main characters, setting, main events, the problem and solution. If the child is familiar with the original fairy tale, invite he or she to identify the similarities and differences between the two versions of the story.

5. Encourage the child to use his or her imagination to create fairytale jumbles based on other familiar stories.

6. Give praise! Children learn best in a positive environment.

IF YOU ENJOYED THIS BOOK, WHY NOT TRY ANOTHER TADPOLES: FAIRYTALE JUMBLES STORY?

Goldilocks and the Wolf	*978-0-7787-8023-6 RLB*	*978-0-7787-8034-2 PB*
The Elves and the Emperor	*978-0-7787-8025-0 RLB*	*978-0-7787-8036-6 PB*
Three Pigs and a Gingerbread Man	*978-0-7787-8026-7 RLB*	*978-0-7787-8037-3 PB*

VISIT WWW.CRABTREEBOOKS.COM FOR OTHER CRABTREE BOOKS.